FOR MY FRIENDS IN SNEINTON

First published in 2006
by Hodder Children's Books

First published in paperback in 2007

Text and illustration copyright © Sarah McConnell 2006

Hodder Children's Books
338 Euston Road,
London NW1 3BH

Hodder Children's Books Australia
Level 17/207 Kent Street,
Sydney, NSW 2000

The right of Sarah McConnell to be identified as the author and
illustrator of this Work has been asserted by her in accordance with
the Copyright, Designs and Patents Act 1988.

A catalogue record of this book is available from the British Library.

PB ISBN: 9780340893449
10 9 8 7 6 5 4 3 2

Printed in China

Hodder Children's Books is a division of Hachette Children's Books.

Don't Mention Pirates

SARAH McCONNELL

h

*Hodder
Children's
Books*

A division of Hachette Children's Books

Scarlet Silver
had a secret that
nobody could guess:

not her mum,

not her dad,

not her brother Cedric,

not even Grandpa Jack...

Now the Silvers were
a very ordinary family –
except that they lived in
a ship-shaped house.

Yes, really **ship shaped.**

Scarlet's mum inherited it from
her famous pirate Grandma...

There was one rule in the Silver house – and only one rule:

Don't mention Pirates, on account of the terrible luck that befell Grandma Silver when she was accidentally eaten by a giant shrimp!

OOPS!

From that day onwards,
No Pirates was the rule.

But that wasn't easy for Scarlet...

...because secretly she wanted to be a **pirate!**

Scarlet loved the smell of sea air.

And was excellent at making people walk the plank.

She'd even taught
Bluebeard her
budgie to squawk,

'Pieces
    of Eight'.

But Mum and Dad were not proud. 'Don't mention pirates,'
they said very loud.

The thing that all pirates, including
Scarlet, loved best was

searching for treasure.

So Mr Silver built Scarlet a treasure detector.

She found odds and ends and bits and bobs, but nothing exciting.

Until one Tuesday, beep, beep, beep, the detector went off!

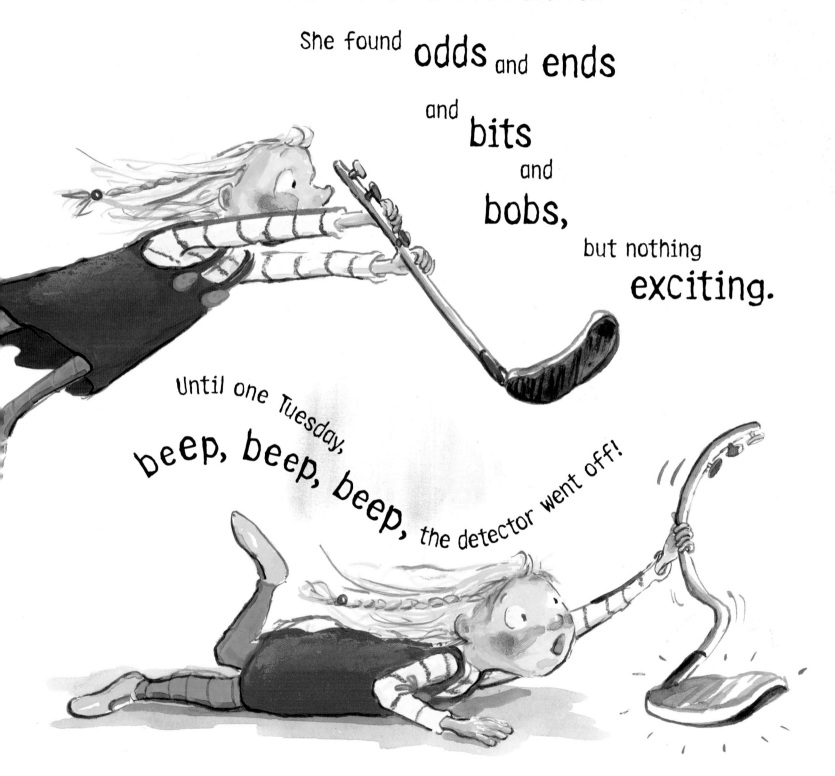

'Bless my barnacles,'
said Scarlet.
'I've found `gold!`'

And she ran into the house
to tell the others.

'It can't be real gold,' said Dad Silver.
'Yes, it can,' said Mum.
'Eureka!' shouted Cedric.
'Fetch Grandpa,' said Scarlet, so excited she
forgot he'd gone fishing with one-eyed Scott.

They all jumped up and started to search
for something, anything to dig up the gold.

They began to dig and the sun beat down so they tied handkerchiefs around their heads.

Hmmm, just what **pirates** wear, thought Scarlet.

At six o'clock, they had a break: ship-shaped biscuits on a ship-shaped plate.

Ahaa, just what **pirates** eat, thought Scarlet.

They carried on digging,
till the sun went down.
'Bedtime,' said Scarlet, yawning.
'Not till we find the loot!' said Cedric.

Ha ha, just how **pirates**
speak, thought Scarlet,
and left them to it.

The next morning, Scarlet got a shock!
'Why are you wearing eye-patches?'
she demanded.
'We were having a mud fight,' replied Mum.
'Aye, and these make perfect eye
protectors,' added Dad.

But Scarlet wasn't fooled.
'You look just like—'

'Don't
    mention
        pirates,'

the others roared.

The Silvers dug and dug, until they could dig no more.

'There must be more gold,' said Dad.
'Aye!' agreed Mum.
'It'll be there,' said Cedric,
pointing to just below the house.
'Wait,' said Scarlet, but they
didn't listen. Dad grabbed his spade.

'Knock it off, ye landlubbers!'
shouted Scarlet.
'Or the house will fall down.'
'Sufferin' seagulls,' said Mum, Dad and Cedric.
'She's right.'

They staggered inside
and flopped on the couch.
'Well, we've still got the
nugget,' said Scarlet.

Just then the back door flew open.

'Ahoy!' said Grandpa Jack.
'I'm back, what's that
you've got there?'

'You champions,' he said. 'You've found me gold tooth.'
And he popped it, click, back into his mouth.

Before anyone could say a word, Grandpa said,
'What's happened this week, you look just like a bunch of p—'

Suddenly, there was a

CREAK, then a

CRACK,

then a...

...SPLOOSH!

'Pirates, that's what we are,'
said the Silvers. And as soon as
they said it, they knew it was true.

'Hoist the main sails!'
shouted Scarlet.

And off they sailed in
search of treasure, because
that's what pirates do!